I0782111

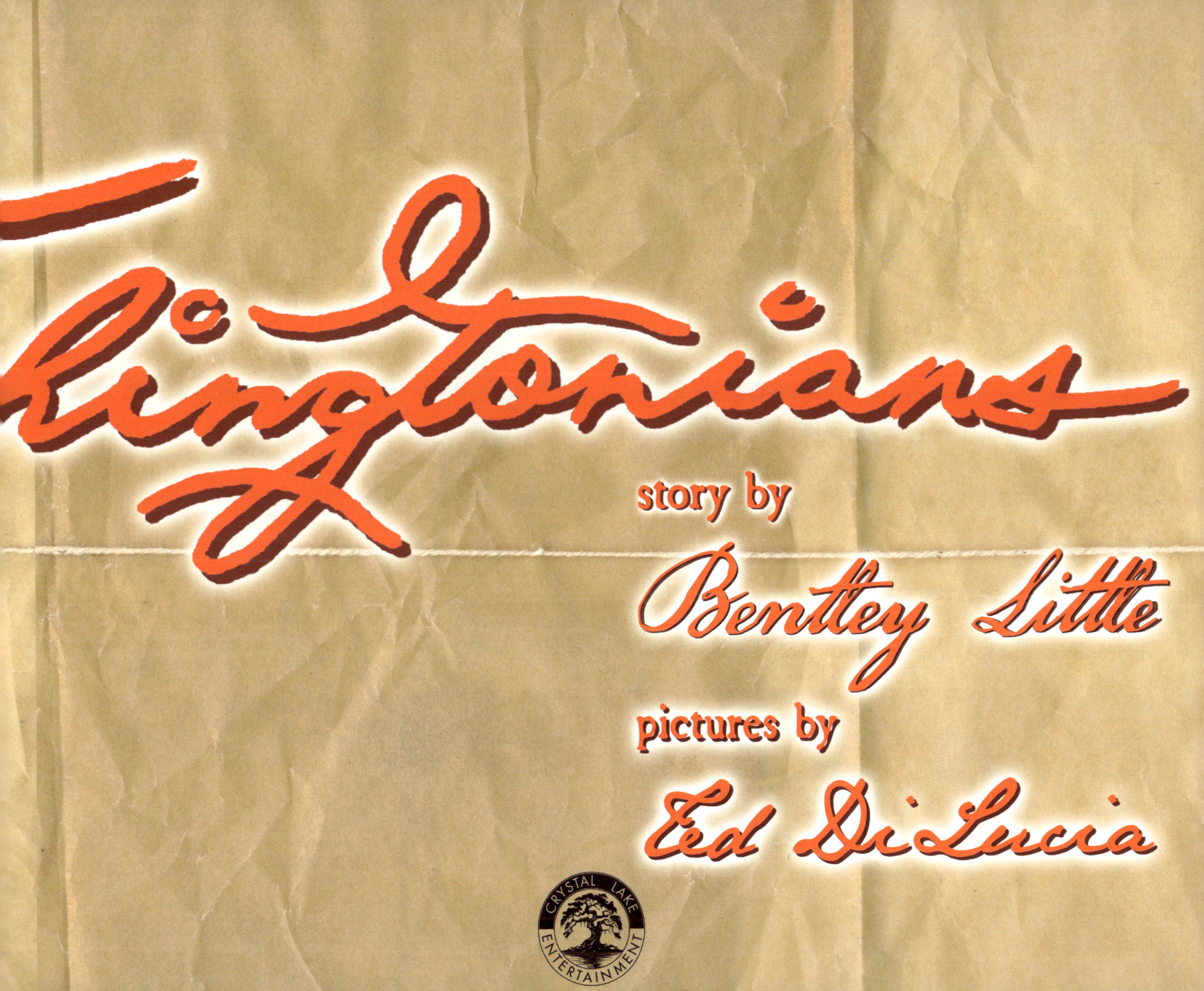
Thingtonians
story by
Bentley Little
pictures by
Ted DiLucia
CRYSTAL LAKE
ENTERTAINMENT

to my fellow patriot

Stephen Gevas

- T.D.

The Washingtonians

"It's authentic," Davis admitted. "It was written by George Washington."

He flipped off the light and, with gloved fingers, removed the parchment manuscript from underneath the magnifier. He shook his head. "Where did you get this? I've never come across anything like it in all my years in the business."

Mike shook his head. "I told you. It was in a trunk of my great-grandmother's stuff that we found hidden in her barn."

"May I ask what you intend to do with it?"

"Well, if it was authentic, we were thinking we'd donate it to the Smithsonian or something. Or sell it to the Smithsonian, if we could. What's the appraisal value of something like this?"

Davis spread his hands in an expansive gesture. "It's invaluable."

"A ballpark figure."

He leaned forward, across the counter. "I'm not Sure you realize what you have here, Mr. Franks. with this one sheet of paper, you can entirely rewrite the history of our country." He paused, letting his words sink in. "History is myth, Mr. Franks. It's not just a collection of names and dates and facts. It's a belief system that ultimately tells more about the people buying into it than it does about the historical participants. What do we retain from our school lessons about George Washington? About Abraham Lincoln? Impressions. Washington was the father of our country. Lincoln freed the slaves. We are who we are as a nation because of what we believe they were. This letter will shatter that belief system and will forever change the image we have of Washington and perhaps all our Founding Fathers. That's a huge responsibility, and I think you should think about it."

"Think about it?"

"Decide if you want to make this knowledge known."

Mike stared at him. "Cover it up? Why? If it's true, then people should know."

"People don't want truth. They want image."

"Yeah, right. How much do I owe you?"

I will skin your children and eat them
upon finishing, I will fashion of their utensils
of their bones.
— ever Yours
G Wash
13 Sep 1777

Philadelphia
free
Washington

FILTER CIGARETTE

"The appraisal fee is fifty dollars." Davis started to write out a receipt, then paused, looked up. "I know a collector," he said. "He's had feelers out for something of this nature for a very long time. Would you mind if I gave him a ring? He's very discreet, very powerful, and, I have reason to believe, very generous."

"No thanks."

"I'd call him for you, set up all the—"

"Not interested," Mike said.

"Very well." Davis returned to the receipt. He finished writing, tore the perforated edge of the paper, and handed Mike a copy.

"But if I may, Mr. Franks, I'd like to suggest you do something."

"What's that?" Mike asked as he took the receipt.

"Sleep on it."

He thought about Washington's letter all the way home. It was lying on the passenger seat beside him, in a protective plastic sleeve that Davis had given him, and he could see it in his peripheral vision, dully reflecting the sun each time he turned north. It felt strange owning something so valuable. He had never had anything this rare in his car before, and it carried with it a lot of responsibility. It made him nervous. He probably should've had it insured before taking it anywhere. What if the car crashed? What if the parchment burned? His hands on the wheel were sweaty. But that wasn't why his hands were sweaty. That wasn't really why he was nervous. No. That was part of it, but the real reason was the note itself.

I will Skin your Children and Eat Them.

The fact that the words had been written by a real person and not a character in a novel would have automatically made him uneasy. But the fact that they had been written by George Washington... Well, that was just too hard to take. There was something creepy about that, something that made a ripple of gooseflesh crawl up the back of his neck each time he looked at the plastic-wrapped brown parchment. He should have felt excited, proud, but instead he felt dirty, oily. He suddenly wished he'd never seen the note. Ahead of him on a billboard above a liquor store, a caricature of George Washington-green, the way he appeared on the dollar bill-was winking at him promoting the high T-bill rate at the Bank of New York. He looked away from the sign, turned down Lincoln Avenue toward home.

Mike paced up and down the length of the kitchen. "He implied that rather than give it to the Smithsonian or something, I should sell it to a private collector who would keep it a secret."

High
T-Bill Rates
Low-Risk
Investment
BNY MELLON
LIQUOR
SAMUEL ADAMS
COORS LIGHT

Pam looked up from the dishes, shook her head. "That's crazy."

"That's what I said."

"Well, don't get too stressed out over it—"

"I'm not getting stressed out."

"Will you let me finish my sentence? I was just going to say, there are a lot of other document appraisers, a lot of museum curators, a lot of university professors. There are a lot of people you can take this to who will know what to do with it."

He nodded, touched her arm. "You're right. I'm sorry. I'm just I don't know. This whole thing has me a little freaked."

"Me too. This afternoon I was helping Amy with her homework. They're studying Johnny Appleseed and George Washington and the cherry tree."

"Two myths."

"There's a picture of Washington in her book ... She shivered, dipped her hands back into the soap suds. "You ought to look at it. It'll give you the willies."

"He smiled at her. "I could give you my willy."

"Later."

"Really creepy, huh?"

"Check it out for yourself."

"I will. You need me in here?"

"No."

He patted the seat of her jeans, gave her a quick kiss on the cheek. "I'll be out front then."

The Birth of American Folklore

JOHNNY APPLESEED

Determined at an early age to devote his life to one purpose: bringing the blessings of apple trees to the new lands in the developing West. His trees brought sweetness to the hard lives of pioneer families and helped sustain them in their labors. Wandering across the West in bare feet and ragged, cast-off clothing, sleeping outdoors, and planting apple seeds wherever he went, Johnny Appleseed took pleasure in denying himself the most basic human comforts in order to carry out his mission. Although legend paints a picture of Johnny as a dreamy wanderer, planting apple seeds throughout the countryside, research reveals him to be a careful, organized businessman, who over a period of nearly fifty years, bought and sold tracts of land and developed thousands of productive apple trees.

THANKSGIVING MYTH

Many white depictions of Thanksgiving hide the conflicts that raged after the settlers arrived. Some Indigenous nations allied with these settlers to aid their own ongoing battles in a time of disease and rebellion. But as the newcomers learned the lay of the land and its farming patterns from their hosts, they intruded upon that land, and the locals lost their lands and cultures.

▲ A WAMPANOAG CHIEF meets the Pilgrims at Plymouth, before relations turned hostile.

George Washington

Alexander Hamilton

Benjamin Franklin

James Madison

Colonial Life

The Cherry Tree Myth

The story goes that when Washington was six years old, he received a hatchet as a gift, after which he promptly went and cut down his father's favorite cherry tree. When his father found out about it, he was understandably angry and confronted his son, asking if he had done it, to which little George replied that yes, indeed, he had done it. And with those brave words, father's anger melted away and he embraced his son, exclaiming that his honesty was worth more than a thousand trees. The Weems' myth went on to be reprinted in the popular McGuffey Reader used by schoolchildren, making it part of American culture, causing Washington's February 22 birthday to be celebrated with cherry dishes, with the cherry often claimed to be a favorite of his.

The famous ride: fact and legend

During the night of April 18–19, 1775, Patriots Paul Revere and William Dawes rode from Boston toward Concord to warn Massachusetts towns that British Redcoats were advancing. Neither Revere nor Dawes actually made it all the way to Concord; they were stopped by British officers. It was a young doctor named Samuel Prescott riding with them who carried the warning to Concord. Little attention was paid to Revere's ride until, some 80 years later, American poet Henry Wadsworth Longfellow wrote "Paul Revere's Ride."

Tall Tales

Grant Wood and the Parson Weems' Fable

Grant Wood was interested in American folklore, as evident in *Parson Weems' Fable*, which shows a young George Washington cutting down a cherry tree. In the right foreground of the painting a white-haired man wears an olive-green, double-breasted coat and looks out at the viewer.

Creating Independence

1840

1845

1850

"All right. I'll be through here in a minute. Go over Amy's math homework, too. Double-check."

"Okay." He walked into the living room. Amy was lying on the floor watching a rerun of Everybody Loves Raymond. Her schoolbook and homework were on the coffee table. He sat down on the couch and was about to pick up the book, when he saw the cover: mountains and clouds and a clipper ship and the Statue of Liberty and the Liberty Bell. The cover was drawn simply, in bright grade school colors, but there was something about the smile on the Statue of Liberty's face that made him realize he did not want to open up the book to see the picture of George Washington.

A commercial came on, and Amy turned around to look at him. "Are you going to check my homework?" she asked.

He nodded. "Yes," he said.

"Do it quick, then. I'm watching TV."

He smiled at her. "Yes, boss."

The pounding woke them up.

It must have been going on for some time, because Amy was standing in the doorway of their bedroom clutching her teddy bear, though she'd supposedly given up the teddy bear two years ago.

Pam gave him a look that let him know how frightened she was, that told him to go out to the living room and find out who the hell was beating on their front door at this time of night, then she was no longer Wife but Mom, and she was out of bed and striding purposefully toward their daughter, telling her in a calm, reasonable, adult voice to go back to bed, that there was nothing the matter. Mike quickly reached down for the jeans he'd abandoned on the floor next to the bed and put them on. The pounding continued unabated, and he felt more than a little frightened himself. But he was Husband and Dad and this was one of those things Husbands and Dads had to do, and he strode quickly out to the living room with a walk and an attitude that made him seem much braver than he actually felt. He slowed down as he walked across the dark living room toward the entryway. Out here, the pounding seemed much louder and much... scarier. There was a strength and will behind the pounding that had not translated across the rooms to the rear of the house and he found himself thinking absurdly that whatever was knocking on the door was not human. It was a stupid thought, an irrational thought, but he stopped at the edge of the entryway nevertheless. The door was solid, there was no window in it, not even a peephole, and he did not want to just open it without knowing who-

what

-was on the other side.

He moved quickly over to the front window. He didn't want to pull the drapes open and draw attention to himself, but he wanted to get a peek at the pounder. There was a small slit where the two halves of the drapes met in the middle of the window, and he bent over to peer through the opening.

Outside on the porch, facing the door, were four men wearing white powdered wigs and satin colonial garb. He thought for a second that he was dreaming. The surrealistic irrationality of this seemed more nightmarish than real. But he saw one of the men pound loudly on the door with his bunched fist, and from the back of the house he heard the muffled sound of Pam's voice as she comforted Amy, and he knew that this was really happening. He should open the door, he knew. He should confront these people. But something about that bunched fist and the look of angry determination on the pounder's face made him hesitate. He was frightened, he realized. More frightened than he had been before he'd peeked through the curtains, when he'd still half thought there might be a monster outside.

I will Skin your Children and Eat Them.

These weirdos were connected somehow to Washington's note. He knew that instinctively. And that was what scared him.

He heard Pam hurrying across the living room toward him, obviously alarmed by the fact that the pounding had not yet stopped. She moved quickly next to him.

"Who is it?" she whispered.

He shook his head. "I don't know."

He peeked again through the split in the curtains, studying the strangers more carefully. She pressed her face next to his. He heard her gasp, felt her pull away.

"Jesus," she whispered. There was fear in her voice. "Look at their teeth." Their teeth?

He focused his attention on the men's mouths. Pam was right. There was something strange about their teeth. He squinted, looked closer.

Their teeth were uniformly yellow. Their teeth were false. George Washington had false teeth. He backed away from the window.

"Call the police," he told Pam. "Now."

"We want the letter!" The voice was strong, filled with an anger and hatred he had not expected. The pounding stopped. "We know you have it, Franks! Give it to us and we will not harm you!"

Mike looked again through the parted curtains. All four of the men were facing the window, staring at him. In the porchlight their skin looked pale, almost corpselike, their eyes brightly fanatic. The man who had been pounding on the door pointed at him. Rage twisted the features of his face. "Give us the letter!"

He wanted to move away, to hide, but Mike forced himself to hold his ground. He was not sure if the men could actually see him through that small slit, but he assumed they could. "I called the police!" he bluffed. "They'll be here any minute!"

The pounder was about to say something but at that second, fate stepped in and there was the sound of a siren coming from somewhere to the east. The men looked confusedly at each other, spoke quietly and quickly between themselves, then began hurrying off the porch. On their arms, Mike saw round silk patches with stylized insignias.

A hatchet and a cherry tree.

"We will be back for you!" one of the men said. "You can't escape!"

"Mom!" Amy called from her bedroom.

"Go get her," Mike said.

"You call the police then."

He nodded as she moved off, but even as he headed toward the phone, he knew with a strange fatalistic certainty that the police would not be able to track down these people, that when these people came back-and they would come back-the police would not be able to protect him and his family. He heard a car engine roar to life, heard tires squealing on the street. He picked up the phone and dialed 911.

He left Pam and Amy home alone the next morning, told them not to answer the door or the telephone and to call the police if they saw any strangers hanging around the neighborhood. He had formulated a plan during the long sleepless hours between the cops' departure and dawn, and he drove to New York University, asking a fresh-faced clerk in administration where the history department was located. Following the kid's directions across campus, he read the posted signs until he found the correct building.

The secretary of the history department informed him that Dr. Hartkinson had his office hours from eight to ten-thirty and was available to speak with him, and he followed her down the hallway to the professor's office. Hartkinson stood upon introduction and shook his hand. He was an elderly man in his mid- to late sixties, with the short stature, spectacles, and whiskers of a Disney movie college professor. "Have a seat," the old man said, clearing a stack of papers from an old straight-backed chair. He thanked the secretary, who retreated down the hall, then moved back behind his oversized desk and sat down himself. "What can I do for you?"

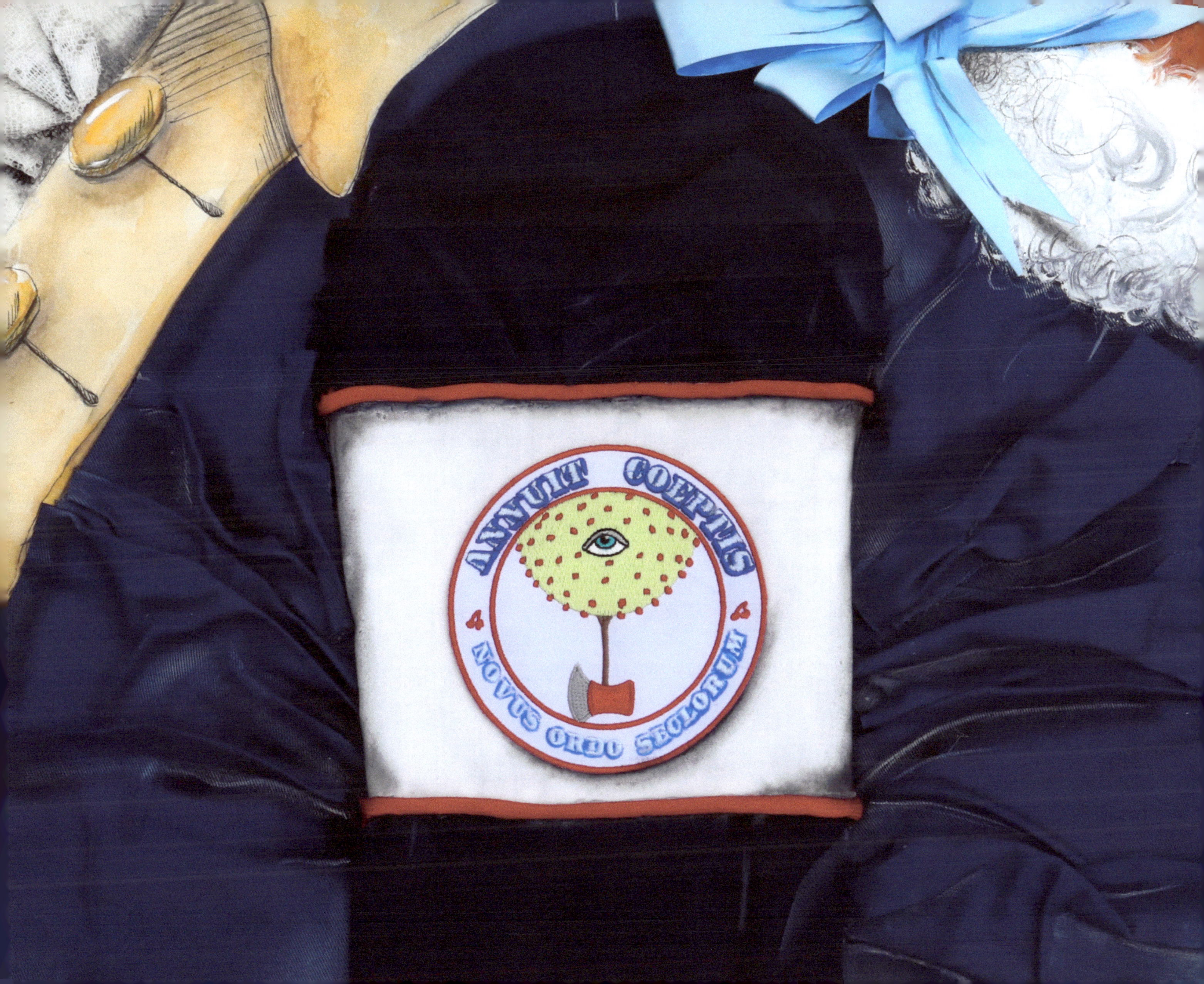

ANNUIT COEPTIS
NOVUS ORDO SEOLORUM

Mike cleared his throat nervously. "I don't really know how to bring this up. It may sound kind of stupid to you, but last night my wife and I were. . . well, we were sleeping, and we were woken up by this pounding on our front door. I went out to investigate, and there were these four men on my porch, calling out my name and threatening me. They were wearing powdered wigs and what looked like Revolutionary War clothes—"

The old man's eyes widened. "Washingtonians!"

"Washingtonians?"

"Shh!" The professor quickly stood and closed his office door. His relaxed, easygoing manner no longer seemed so relaxed and easygoing. There was a tenseness in his movements, an urgency in his walk. He immediately sat back down, took the phone off the hook, and pulled closed his lone window. He leaned conspiratorially across the desk, and when he spoke his voice was low and frightened. "You're lucky you came to me," he said. "They have spies everywhere."

"What?"

"Dr. Gluck and Dr. Cannon, in our history department here, are Washingtonians. Most of the other professors are sympathizers. It's pure luck you talked to me first. What do you have?"

"What?"

"Come on now. They wouldn't have come after you unless you had something they wanted. What is it?

A letter?" Mike nodded dumbly.

"I thought so. What did this letter say?"

Mike reached into his coat pocket and pulled out the piece of parchment.

The professor took the note out of the plastic. He nodded when he'd finished reading. "The truth. That's what's in this letter."

Mike nodded.

"George Washington was a cannibal. He was a fiend and a murderer and a child eater. But he was also chosen to be the father of our country, and that image is more important than the actuality."

ANNUIT COEPTIS
NOVUS ORDO SECLORUM
Fig. 1.
Dr. Samuel Su
Cherry Tree Ins
New York University
1962
TONIGHT
WEIRD FANTASY

"Someone else told me that."

"He was right." The professor shifted in his seat. "Let me tell you something about historians. Historians, for the most part, are not interested in truth. They are not interested in learning facts and teaching people what really happened. They want to perpetuate the lies they are sworn to defend. It's an exclusive club, the people who know why our wars were really fought, what really happened behind the closed doors of our world's leaders, and most of them want to keep it that way. There are a few of us altruists, people like myself who got into this business to learn and share our learning. But the majority of historians are PR people for the past." He thought for a moment. "Benjamin Franklin did not exist. Did you know that? He never lived. He was a composite character created for mass consumption. It was felt by the historians that a character was needed who would embody America's scientific curiosity, boldness of vision, and farsighted determination, who would inspire people to reach for greatness in intellectual endeavors. So they came up with Franklin, an avuncular American Renaissance man. Americans wanted to believe in Franklin, wanted to believe that his qualities were their qualities, and they bought into the concept lock, stock, and barrel, even falling for that absurd kite story.

"It was the same with Washington. Americans wanted him to be the father of our country, needed him to be the father of our country, and they were only too happy to believe what we historians told them."

Mike stared at Hartkinson, then looked away toward the rows of history books on the professor's shelves. These were the men who had really determined our country's course, he realized. The historians. They had altered the past and affected the future. It was not the great men who shaped the world, it was the men who told of the great men who shaped the world.

"You've stumbled upon something here," Hartkinson said. "And that's why they're after you. That note's like a leak from Nixon's White House, and the President's going to do everything in his power to make damn sure it goes no further than you. Like I said, the history biz isn't anything like it appears on the outside. It's a weird world in here, weird and secretive. And the Washingtonians... " He shook his head, "They're the fringe of the fringe. And they are a very dangerous group indeed."

"They all had wooden teeth, the ones who came to my house——"

"Ivory, not wood. That's one of those little pieces of trivia they're very adamant about getting out to the public. The original core group of Washingtonians screwed up on that one, and subsequent generations have felt that the impression that was created made Washington out to be a weak buffoon. They've had a hard time erasing that 'wooden teeth' image, though."

"Is that how you can spot them? Their teeth?"

"No. They wear modern dentures when they're not in uniform. They're like the Klan in that respect."

fake news

"Only in that respect?"

The professor met his eyes. "No."

"What. . ." He cleared his throat. "What will they try to do to me?"

"Kill you. And eat you."

Mike stood. "Jesus fucking Christ. I'm going to the police with this. I'm not going to let them terrorize my family—"

"Now just hold your horses there. That's what they'll try to do to you. If you listen to me, and if you do exactly what I say, they won't succeed." He looked at Mike, tried unsuccessfully to smile. "I'm going to help you. But you'll have to tell me a few things first. Do you have any children? Any daughters?"

"Yes. Amy."

"This is kind of awkward. Is she. . . a virgin?"

"She's ten years old!"

The professor frowned. "That's not good."

"Why isn't it good?"

"Have you see the insignia they wear on their arms?"

"The hatchet and the cherry tree?"

"Yes."

"What about it?"

"That was Professor Summerlin's contribution. The Washingtonians have always interpreted the cherry tree story as a cannibal allegory, a metaphoric retelling of Washington's discovery of the joys of killing people and eating their flesh. To take it a step further, Washington's fondness for the meat of virgins is well documented, and that's what made Professor Summerlin think of the patch. He simply updated the symbol to include the modern colloquial definition of 'cherry.'"

AMY FRANKS

Mike understood what Hartkinson meant, and he felt sick to his stomach.

"They all like virgin meat," the professor said.

"I'm going to the police. Thanks for your help and all, but I don't think you can——"

The door to the office was suddenly thrown open, and there they stood: four men and one woman dressed in Revolutionary garb. Mike saw yellowish teeth in smiling mouths.

"You should have known better, Julius," the tallest man said, pushing his way into the room.

"Run!" Hartkinson yelled.

Mike tried to, making a frill-bore, straight-ahead dash toward the door, but he was stopped by the line of unmoving Washingtonians. He'd thought he'd be able to break through, to knock a few of them over and take off down the hall, but evidently they had expected that and were prepared.

Two of the men grabbed Mike and held him.

"My wife'll call the police if I'm not back in time."

"Who cares?" the tall man said.

"They'll publish it!" Mike yelled in desperation. "I gave orders for them to publish the letter if anything happened to me! If I was even late.

The woman looked at him calmly. "No, you didn't."

"Yes, I did. My wife'll——"

"We have your wife," she said.

A stab of terror flashed through him. She smiled at him, nodding. "And your daughter."

237
DR. HARTKINSON
LETTERS

He was not sure where they were taking him, but wherever it was, it was far. Although he was struggling as they hustled him out of the building and into their van, no one tried to help him or tried to stop them. A few onlookers smiled indulgently, as though they were witnessing the rehearsal of a play or a staged publicity stunt, but that was the extent of the attention they received. If only they hadn't been wearing those damn costumes, Mike thought. His abduction wouldn't have looked so comical if they'd been dressed in terrorist attire.

He was thrown into the rear of the van, the door was slammed shut, and a few seconds later the engine roared to life and they were off.

They drove for hours. There were no windows in the back of the van, and he could not tell in which direction they were traveling, but after a series of initial stops and starts and turns, the route straightened out, the speed became constant, and he assumed they were moving along a highway.

When the van finally stopped and the back door was opened and he was dragged out, it was in the country, in a wooded, meadow area that was unfamiliar to him. Through the trees he saw a building, a white, green-trimmed colonial structure that he almost but not quite recognized. The Washingtonians led him away from the building to a small shed. The shed door was opened, and he saw a dark tunnel and a series of steps leading down. Two of the Washingtonians went before him, the other three remained behind him, and in a group they descended the stairway.

Mt. Vernon, Mike suddenly realized. The building was Mt. Vernon, George Washington's home. The steps ended at a tunnel, which wound back in the direction of the building and ended in a large warehouse-sized basement that looked as if it had been converted into a museum of the Inquisition. They were underneath Mt. Vernon, he assumed, in what must have been Washington's secret lair.

"Where's Pam?" he demanded. "Where's Amy?"

"You'll see them," the woman said.

The tall man walked over to a cabinet, pointed at the dull ivory objects inside. "These are spoons carved entirely from the femurs of the First Continental Congress." He gestured toward an expensively framed painting hanging above the cabinet. The painting, obviously done by one of early America's finer artists, depicted a blood-spattered George Washington, flanked by two naked and equally blood-spattered women, devouring a screaming man. "Washington commissioned this while he was president."

The man seemed eager to show off the room's possessions, and Mike wondered if he could use that somehow to get an edge, to aid in an escape attempt. He was still being held tightly by two of the Washingtonians, and though he had not tried breaking out of their grip since entering the basement, he knew he would not be able to do so.

The tall man continued to stare reverently at the painting. "He acquired the taste during the winter when he and his men were starving and without supplies or reinforcements. The army began to eat its dead, and Washington found that he liked the taste. During the long days, he carved eating utensils and small good luck fetishes from the bones of the devoured men. Even after supplies began arriving, he continued to kill a man a day for his meals."

"He began to realize that with the army in his control, he was in a position to call the shots," the woman explained from behind him. "He could create a country of cannibals. A nation celebrating and dedicated to the eating of human flesh!"

Mike turned his head, looked at her. "He didn't do it, though, did he?" He shook his head. "You people are so full of crap."

"You won't think so when we eat your daughter's kidneys."

Anger coursed through him and Mike tried to jerk out of his captors' grasps. The men's grips tightened, and he soon gave up, slumping back in defeat.

The tall man ran a hand lovingly over the top of a strange tablelike contraption in the middle of the room. "This is where John Hancock was flayed alive," he said. "His blood anointed this wood. His screams sang in these chambers."

"You're full of shit."

"Am I?" He looked dreamily around the room. "Jefferson gave his life for us, you know. Sacrificed himself right here, allowed Washingtonians to rip him apart with their teeth. Franklin donated his body to us after death—"

"There was no Benjamin Franklin."

The man smiled, showing overly white teeth. "So you know."

"Shouldn't you be wearing your wooden. choppers?"

The man punched him in the stomach, and Mike, doubled over, pain flaring in his abdomen, his lungs suddenly unable to draw in enough breath.

"You are not a guest," the man said. "You are a prisoner. Our prisoner. For now." He smiled. "Later you may be supper."

Mike closed his eyes, tried not to vomit. When he could again breathe normally, he looked up at the man. "Why this James Bond shit? You going to give me your whole fucking history before you kill me? You going to explain all of your toys to me and hope I admire them? Fuck you! Eat me, you sick assholes!"

The woman grinned. "Don't worry. We will."

A door opened at the opposite end of the room, and Pam and Amy were herded in by three new Washingtonians. His daughter and wife looked white and frightened. Amy was crying, and she cried even harder when she saw him.

"Daddy!" she screamed.

"Lunch," the tall man said. "Start up the barbecue."

The Washingtonians laughed.

The woman turned to Mike. "Give us the letter," she said.

"And you'll let me go? Yeah. Right."

Where was the letter? he wondered. Hartkinson had had it last. Had he destroyed it or ditched it somewhere, like a junkie flushing drugs down the toilet after the arrival of the cops?

And where was Hartkinson? Why hadn't they kidnapped him, too?

He was about to ask just that very question when there was the sound of scuffling from the door through which Pam and Amy had entered. All of the Washingtonians turned to face that direction.

And there was Hartkinson. He was dressed in a red British Revolutionary War uniform, and behind him stood a group of other redcoats clutching bayonets. A confused and frightened youth, who looked like a tour guide, peered into the room from behind them.

"Unhand those civilians!" Hartkinson demanded in an affected British accent.

He and his friends looked comical in their shabby mis-matched British uniforms, but they also looked heroic, and Mike's adrenaline started pumping as they burst through the doorway. There were a lot of them, he saw, fifteen or twenty, and they outnumbered the Washingtonians more than two to one.

Two of the Washingtonians drew knives and ran toward Pam and Amy.

"No!" Mike yelled.

Musket balls cut the men down in midstride.

Mike took a chance and tried his escape tactic again. Either the men holding him were distracted or their grip had simply weakened after all this time, but he successfully jerked out of their hands, broke away, and turned and kicked one of the men hard in the groin. The other man moved quickly out of his way, but Mike didn't care. He ran across the room, past arcane torture devices, to Pam and Amy.

"Attack!" someone yelled. The fight began. It was mercifully short. Mike heard gunfire, heard ricochets, heard screams, saw frenzied moveme but he kept his head low and knew nothing of the specifics of what was happening. All he knew was that by the time he reached Pam and Am they were free. He stood up from his crouch, looked around the room, and saw instantly that most of the Washingtonians were dead or capture The tall man was lying on the floor with a dark crimson stain spreading across his powder blue uniform, and that made Mike feel good. Served the bastard right.

N. E.
V. M.
DIE

established
themselves by
absolute
of the thirteen united
Declaration

States of
effected tord
our laws
1776

Both Pam and Amy were hugging each other and crying, and he hugged them too and found that he was crying as well. He felt a light tap on his shoulder and instinctively whirled around, fists clenched, but it was only Hartkinson.

Mike stared at him for a moment, blinked. "Thank you," he said, and he began crying anew, tears of relief. "Thank you."

The professor nodded, smiled. There were flecks of blood in his white Disney beard. "Leave," he said. "You don't want to see what comes next."

"But—"

His voice was gentle. "The Washingtonians aren't the only ones with. . . different traditions."

"You're not cannibals, too?"

"No, but. . . " He shook his head. "You'd better go."

Mike looked at Pam and Amy, and nodded.

From inside his red coat, Hartkinson withdrew a piece of parchment wrapped in plastic. The letter. "Take it to the Smithsonian. Tell the world." His voice was low and filled with reverence. "It's history."

"Are you going to be okay here?"

"We've done this before." He gestured toward the tour guide, who was still standing in the corner. "He'll show you the way out." He shook his head, smiling ruefully. "The history biz is not like it appears from the outside."

"I guess not." Mike put his arm around Pam, who in turn pulled Amy toward the door. The tour guide, white-faced, started slowly up the steps.

"Don't look back," Hartkinson advised.

Mike waved his acquiescence and began walking up the stairs, clutching Washington's letter. Behind them, he heard screams-cries of terror, cries of pain-and though he didn't want to, though he knew he shouldn't, he smiled as he led his family out of the basement and into Washington's home above.

V.
M.
N. E.

is a former member of a popular 1990s boy band, and currently works as a prison custodian in Alabama. Bentley Little's hobbies are writing horror stories and training Sea Monkeys to swim around magic rocks.

is an artist whose other works include the picture book based on Joe R. Lansdale's short story classic <u>Incident On and Off a Mountain Road</u>. DiLucia is a graduate from the Rhode Island School of Design, and is the only witchdoctor still practicing medicine at Women & Infants Hospital.